WHO

WRITTEN BY RICHARD THOMPSON
ILLUSTRATED BY MARTIN SPRINGETT

ORCA BOOK PUBLISHERS

If you go to the forest and try to call an owl by name — if, for instance, you call, "Bartholomew! Bartholomew! Are you there?" a voice may answer back. And that voice will say,

"Whoooo?"

And that is because owls do not have names.

But there was a time, long ago, when owls called each other by name just as you and I do. In that time, there lived two owls named Bartholomew and Eleanor, and they had three children.

When their first child was born, they decided to name the hatchling Night. "Our daughter will grow to be a stealthy hunter," Bartholomew said. "We will name her Night, for no hunter steals through the forest more quietly than Night does."

The girl was called Night, and Night, the bringer of darkness, was pleased when he heard it. He sent the owlet a present — a night-dark cloak embroidered with stars.

When their second child was born, Bartholomew declared, "We will name this child Moon, for she will grow to be a great beauty, and in all the forest nothing can rival the radiant beauty of the Moon."

The girl was called Moon. And Moon who lives in the sky was flattered when she heard it. She sent the infant owl a present — a mirror of fragile crystal.

And in time a third child, a son, was born to Bartholomew and Eleanor. "This boy shall grow to great wisdom and will be the keeper of many secrets," Eleanor told their friends. "We shall name him Tomorrow after the greatest keeper of secrets."

And so the boy was called Tomorrow. And he who no one really knows was flattered when he heard it. He sent the child a present — a box with a golden lock and key in which to keep his secrets.

The owlets grew, in time, to owlhood. As they grew, the forest animals spoke of them in awed whispers.

"Beware of the owl called Night," warned Squirrel. "She hunts on silent wings."

"We are very beautiful with our painted wings," said Butterfly, "but not nearly as beautiful as the owl called Moon."

"I know many of the secrets of the forest," said Snake, "but no one knows what secrets the owl called Tomorrow has locked away in his box."

Sadly, the young owls believed all the wonderful things the other animals said about them . . .

Night Owl pulled her cloak around herself and spoke in dangerous whispers. "I am not only the stealthiest hunter in the forest, I am more stealthy even than Night, for whom I was named. The bringer of darkness always gives warning of his approach in the brilliant colours of the sunset. But no one knows when I am coming."

Moon Owl stroked her feathers and murmured, "I am not only the most beautiful creature in the forest, I am more beautiful than Moon, for whom I was named. Her beauty dwindles night by night until she vanishes altogether, but my beauty remains constant."

Tomorrow looked out at the forest from under hooded eyes and said softly, "I have secrets locked away that even Tomorrow, for whom I was named, will never share. And when Tomorrow gives away his secrets to Today, as he must, I will still have mine."

Echoes of the owls' boastful words reached Night, the bringer of darkness, and Moon, who lives in the sky, and Tomorrow, whom no one really knows. They were angry.

"These scamps shall learn a lesson," Night growled. Moon and Tomorrow agreed.

When Night next came to the forest, Moon stayed at home, even though she was at her fullest and most brilliant. Night turned his cloak inside out so that no one could see the stars. The forest was inky dark. Even the keenest sighted animals could not see to move.

"Never mind," said all the animals, "everything will be fine when Tomorrow comes."

But Tomorrow didn't come.

The animals became very hungry and thirsty, but still they dared not venture out into the absolute darkness.

Finally one brave mouse crept from her hole and, feeling her way carefully across the forest floor, made her way to the owls' tree. "Night Owl," she called, "the light has been hidden from us, but you can find it if any hunter can."

Night Owl crept out onto the branch in front of the nest and looked at the impenetrable darkness. The blackness filled her with a dread she had never felt before. She turned silently and slid back along the branch. As she went, her cloak caught on a twig and pulled from her shoulders. It fluttered down through the blackness and was never seen again.

"Moon Owl," called the mouse, "come and let your beauty light the forest."

The beautiful young owl crept out onto the branch in front of the nest. But her beauty and the mouse's simple homeliness were equally invisible in the great blackness. Moon Owl wondered if she had disappeared. As she lifted her mirror to check, it slipped from her grasp and shattered on the ground below the tree.

"Tomorrow Owl," called the mouse, "please come and use your wisdom to bring light to the forest."

Bartholomew and Eleanor's son dragged his box out of the nest and in the great blackness fumbled with the lock. The key slipped from his claws and fell to the forest floor. No one will ever know for sure if the young owl had a secret in that box that would have brought the light they sought, for the key was lost forever amongst the ferns.

The mouse began to cry softly. When Eleanor heard her tiny sobs, she said, "Bartholomew, you must speak to the bringer of darkness. Perhaps he will listen to you."

Bartholomew stepped carefully out onto the branch and called to Night, "My friend, why are you angry with us? Where is Moon? Why doesn't Tomorrow come?"

Night replied, "Bartholomew Owl, when you gave our names to your children, we were pleased and flattered. But your children have forgotten who they are. For all their stealth and beauty and wisdom, they are, after all, animals among animals, and they must remember that. We have decided. We want our names back!"

"But what will we call our children?" cried Bartholomew.

"That is your problem," said Night. "If you want Moon and Tomorrow to return to the forest, you will give us our names back."

Fortunately, Night could not see the anger that flashed in Bartholomew's eyes, nor hear the protest that shouted in his heart. And Bartholomew, being somewhat wiser than his children, answered as he knew he must.

"It will be done."

Reluctantly, Bartholomew told his children they had to give back their wonderful names. And, reluctantly, they did.

Tomorrow came to the forest and the animals could see to hunt for food and water. When Night came again, Moon came with him. And all was as it should be again.

But Bartholomew did not share in the rejoicing that filled the forest. His children had been robbed to ransom the light, and, though he had no choice but to pay the ransom, he was determined that the sacrifice would be remembered.

"If my children cannot have the names they deserve," he declared, "they shall have no names at all."

And that is why, to this very day, owls do not have names.

So if you go to the forest and try to call an owl by name . . .

Text copyright © 1993 Richard Thompson
Illustration copyright © 1993 Martin Springett

Publication assistance provided by The Canada Council

Canadian Cataloguing in Publication Data
Thompson, Richard, 1951 –
Who

ISBN 0-920501-98-2
1. Owls — Juvenile fiction.   I. Springett,
Martin.   II. Title.
PS8589.H53W56 1993   jC813'.54   C93-091562-3
PZ7.T56wn 1993

Orca Book Publishers   **Orca Book Publishers**
PO Box 5626, Station B   1574 Gulf Road, Box 3028
Victoria, BC   V8R 6S4   Point Roberts, WA   98281
Canada   USA

Book design by Christine Toller & Martin Springett
Printed and bound in Hong Kong